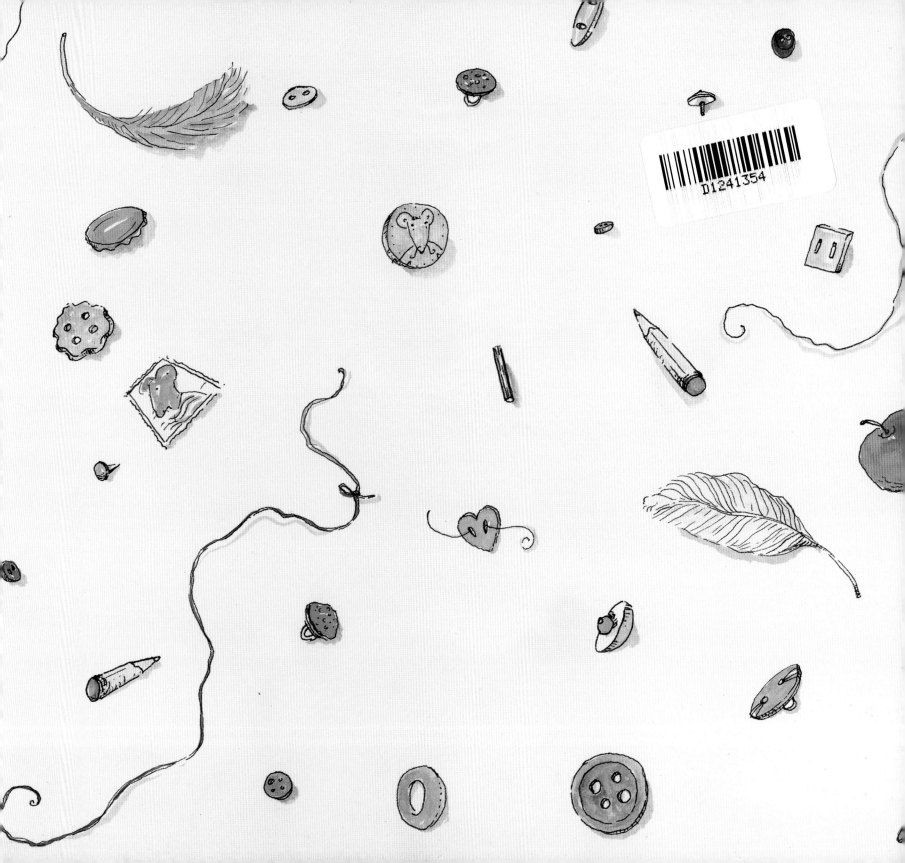

A Friend Like Ed

Karen Wagner • Illustrations by Janet Pedersen

walker and Company ⊛ New York

To Emmy, who gives me wings —K. W.

For Mom and Dad —J. P.

First published in the United States of America in 1998 by
Walker Publishing Company, Inc.

Published simultaneously in Canada by Thomas Allen & Son Canada,
Limited, Markham, Ontario.

Library of Congress Cataloging-in-Publication Data
Wagner, Karen.
A friend like Ed/Karen Wagner; illustrations by Janet Pedersen.
p. cm.
Summary: Mildred accepts her best friend, Ed, even though he is
sometimes eccentric.
ISBN 0-8027-8662-6. —ISBN 0-8027-8663-4 (reinforced)
[1. Mice—Fiction. 2. Best friends—Fiction. 3. Friendship—Fiction.]
I. Pedersen, Janet, ill. II. Title.
PZ7.W12428Fr 1998

98-14311
[E]—dc21
CIP
AC

Book design by Janet Pedersen

Printed in Hong Kong

10 9 8 7 6 5 4 3 2

Mildred and **Ed** had been friends for as long as anyone could remember . . . even though some thought Ed a bit unusual.

And Mildred had to admit that Ed did have some strange hobbies.

Still, no one could hold a candle to Ed's homemade, fudge-frosted, triple-layer cake. Or make Mildred laugh so hard her eyes would water.

One Saturday morning Mildred said, "Let's try something different."

"Like what?" asked Ed.

"How about poetry? It's so romantic," answered Mildred.

"Okay," said Ed.

Sunset is beautiful orange and purple.
Early evening looks so . . .
yurple?

What's "yurple"?

Is "yurple" a word?

Ed was the surprise hit of the poetry class. He could find a rhyme for anything.

Leaves are falling
Winter's calling,
Before you know
There will be snow,
So let us shout hurray
For this warm and sunny day.

Here is a poem
all about brushing.
You should do it,
don't think about rushing.
For it would be a loss
if you forgot to floss.

And anyplace was the right place for a poem.

we love to eat,
we don't use our feet.
I like bread,
but not on my head.
For dessert I'd like some pie,
Banana cream I think I'll try.

Lemon yellow
little fellow.
You are sour
every hour.
Come along
with me,
I'll put you
in my tea.

One day at the market, Ed stopped
in the middle of aisle three for a poem.
Mildred felt eyes peering up from the pears.
She heard snickering from behind the
snowpeas. She sensed giggling going on
by the grapes.

Mildred was so embarrassed that she
tiptoed backward out of the store,
hoping no one would notice that
she was Ed's friend.

That night Mildred dreamed that her room was filled with Ed's button collection. Buttons on the floor, buttons on the chair, buttons on the walls, buttons everywhere. Then she dreamed she was ice-skating, wearing a fancy dress. People oohed and aahed as they watched her skate.

The next day Mildred went to the ice-skating rink. She held tightly to the side because her knees wobbled. That was when she first saw Pearl. Pearl was in the middle of the rink spinning around and around. Mildred was sure no one could ever think Pearl was unusual in any odd sort of way. And she was positive Pearl had never recited poetry.

"C -c -could you teach me how to do that?" Mildred stammered.

"Of course," Pearl replied. "I can do anything. And I can do it better than anyone else."

Autumn blew in like a wind.
Ed sat on top of the hill and watched
the squirrels gather acorns.

Pearl invited Mildred to
a costume party. "We will
go as a huge dragon,"
Pearl announced.

Pearl made a very
impressive dragon.
Mildred had a hard time
seeing and an even
harder time eating.

When winter came, Mildred and Pearl went skating on the
pond. Pearl said, "Wanna see me do a triple twirl?"

"Maybe I'm ready to learn that," Mildred said.

"I think today you should just watch," Pearl said.

Ed made a fudge-frosted, triple-layer cake, even though he
knew it would take forever to eat it by himself.

One morning Pearl showed Mildred all of her ice-skating awards. Then she took out her photo albums.

"Wasn't I the cutest baby you ever saw?" Pearl asked as she turned the pages. Mildred was busy staring out the window at a tree. It had round, sparkling drops of ice that looked like hundreds of buttons.

Winter was long. Ed sorted buttons by color. He sorted buttons by size.

Late at night he pulled the covers up around him. He was wishing for spring, and secretly, in a voice no one could hear, he was wishing for Mildred.

When the first snow fell, Pearl and Mildred went sledding. Pearl wore her new purple scarf with matching mittens and hat. She sat on the sled and stretched out her legs.

"Where will I sit?" Mildred asked.

"I will sled down the hill," Pearl said, "and you can sled up."

Mildred felt a lump in her throat. "I'm not sledding up," she said. "I'm going home."

"Fine," Pearl said, and disappeared down the hill.

The next day Mildred woke up with a sweet tooth. "There's nothing I want except fudge-frosted, triple-layer cake," she thought. "No one could ever make a cake the way Ed can, but I will just have to try."

Mildred looked in the pantry only to find some jars of this and cans of that but nothing that would make a fudge-frosted, triple-layer cake. So, Mildred decided to go to the market.

It was cold—the kind of cold that chills you from the inside out. Mildred dressed in the very warmest clothes she could find until only a tiny bit of her face was showing, then she set off for town.

Snow blew in Mildred's face. The wind howled. She was about to pass by the pond when she saw someone. "Who in the world would be skating on a day like today?" she wondered.

Whoever it was, he was not very good. But there was
something familiar about the way he stumbled along.
"Ed!" thought Mildred, and she hid behind a tree.

Ed began to skate back and forth in a most odd manner.
"What could he be doing?" Mildred wondered.
After Ed left, Mildred peered over at the ice.

Ed was working on a new invention for
picking string beans when the doorbell rang.

There was no one there, but on the stoop he saw a small box and a note.
He carefully opened the box. Inside was a pen.
The note said:

Dear Ed,
You may think this is a pen, but it is not.
It is a thousand poems waiting to be written.
It is a pair of wings to help you fly.
Love, Mildred

Ed knocked on Mildred's kitchen door. Mildred was putting the finishing touches on a very lopsided fudge-frosted, triple-layer cake.

Ed felt suddenly shy. He looked down at his sneakers.

"Thank you for the pen," he said.

Mildred blushed, "I wanted to write you a poem, but I didn't know how. I guess I need lessons."

"But you did write me a poem," Ed said. "The best kind, one from the heart. That's the only lesson there is."

Mildred stood on the kitchen chair.

"Ed, oh, Ed
Don't ever go.
Ed, oh, Ed
I missed you so.
Ed, oh, Ed
what would I do . . ."

Ed interrupted. "Don't worry, Mildred,
you're my best friend, too."